Mikale of Hawaii

BY MAYA ANGELOU
ILLUSTRATED BY LIZZY ROCKWELL

A Random House PICTUREBACK® Book

RANDOM HOUSE 🏠 NEW YORK

Text copyright © 2004 by Maya Angelou. Illustrations copyright © 2004 by Lizzy Rockwell. All rights reserved under International and Pan-American Copyright Conventions. Published in the United States by Random House Children's Books, a division of Random House, Inc., New York, and simultaneously in Canada by Random House of Canada Limited, Toronto.
www.randomhouse.com/kids
Library of Congress Cataloging-in-Publication Data
Angelou, Maya. Mikale of Hawaii / by Maya Angelou ; illustrated by Lizzy Rockwell. — 1st ed.   p.   cm. — (A Random House pictureback)
SUMMARY: Mikale, a young Hawaiian boy, learns to swim with help from his uncle.
ISBN 0-375-82835-4 (trade) — ISBN 0-375-92835-9 (lib. bdg.)
[1. Fear—Fiction. 2. Swimming—Fiction. 3. Uncles—Fiction. 4. Hawaii—Fiction.] I. Rockwell, Lizzy, ill. II. Title. III. Series.
PZ7.A5833Mi 2004 [E]—dc22 2003025077
Printed in the United States of America   First Edition   10 9 8 7 6 5 4 3 2 1
PICTUREBACK, RANDOM HOUSE, and the Random House colophon are registered trademarks of Random House, Inc.

When I was a little girl,
I looked around at my world.
It was small, so was I.
Then my world began to grow
With each child I came to know.
Now I try,
Now I dare
To make a new friend
Everywhere.

Let me tell you about my friend Mikale. He lives on the beautiful island of Oahu in Hawaii with his parents, his baby sister Leilani, and a pet fish. One day, Mikale's fish told me a story. You may not know that fish can talk, but they are good storytellers if you listen closely. And now I will tell you the story that Keiki'la the fish told me. . . .

You see, Mikale had the same nickname as his fish—Keiki'la—meaning that he was part boy, part fish. Of course he wasn't, but he *did* swim very well. This was not always so. When Mikale was younger, he was afraid of the ocean.

Every time his family went to a luau (which is a Hawaiian feast) by the shore, Mikale begged to stay in the car. His mother would kiss him and say, "Come now." His father would have to carry him down to the beach.

Mikale would sit in the sand and play with seashells. Sometimes his father would take him by the hand and they would walk along the beach or sometimes they would stop and make sand castles.

But still Mikale wouldn't go in the water.

Then Uncle Mako came to visit. He was a champion swimmer. He looked straight into Mikale's eyes and asked, "Are *you* the boy who is afraid of the ocean?"

Embarrassed, Mikale said, "Yes."

"I brought you a gift," said Uncle Mako. "Come and see."

In the living room was a fish tank with one small fish in it. He said, "This is Keiki'la. You must feed him, keep his water fresh, and talk to him every day."

"What would I say?" Mikale wanted to know.

"Just tell him why you are afraid of the ocean and listen to what he says. He knows more about swimming than I do," said Uncle Mako.

The next day, Mikale's uncle took him to a swimming pool and asked him if he was afraid of the water in a bathtub.

"No!" Mikale answered, giggling.

Then he asked whether Mikale was afraid of the pool. "A little," Mikale said.

"Well," said Uncle Mako. "This is where we'll start. Just think of it as a big bathtub."

Uncle Mako jumped off the diving board and did two flips. Then he swam up and down the pool. When he came up for air, he asked, "Do you believe I can swim well enough to protect you?"

Mikale nodded yes.

Uncle Mako held Mikale's hand as he stepped into the shallow end.

"Get on my back and put your arms around my neck. I'll swim a few laps with you." He ducked under the water so Mikale could climb on.

Uncle Mako swam back and forth until Mikale felt as though *he* was doing the swimming. It was fun!

That first day, Mikale learned to tread water. That is where you kick and kick your legs to stay afloat. Uncle Mako also taught Mikale how to float on his back and how to put his face in the water and blow out bubbles. Mikale was good at it. He learned that if you are not afraid, water can be your friend.

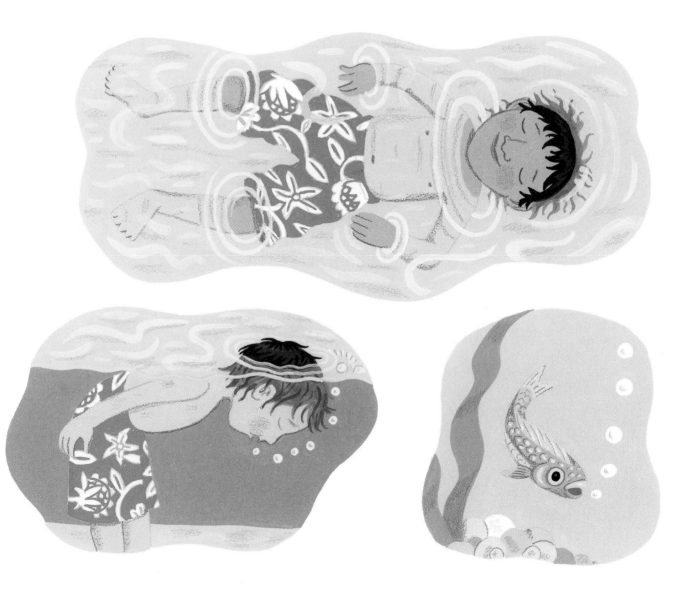

Which is exactly what he told Keiki'la later that day. Then he asked, "What's it like to be a fish?" Keiki'la blew a bubble—*bloop!*—and Mikale knew just what he meant.

The next day at the pool, Uncle Mako introduced Mikale to his friend Annemarie.

"I hear you are doing very well with your swimming lessons," she said. "Come on, Mako. Let's take Mikale for a swim!"

They got on either side of Mikale and held him up so he glided along. He felt very secure. They swam up and down the pool, with Mikale moving his arms and legs as though he was swimming all by himself!

In a few days, he *was* swimming by himself! At first he dog-paddled, and then as the weeks went by, he began to turn his head and breathe the way Uncle Mako had taught him. Mikale felt strong and proud swimming one whole length of the pool as Uncle Mako cheered him on.

That evening, when he told Keiki'la about swimming by himself, Mikale realized he wasn't afraid of the pool anymore! "I think I know what it's like to swim like a fish!" he said. Keiki'la swam around and around happily.

At dinner, Mikale's father and mother clapped for him.
"Mako tells me that you are swimming so well," said
his father.

"I always knew you would learn one day," his mother chimed in. And baby Leilani blew a bubble—*bloop!*—just like Keiki'la.

"This calls for a celebration," said Mikale's mom. "Let's have a luau!"

So the next day, that's just what they did. Uncle Mako and Annemarie came, too.

"Are you ready to go in?" asked Mikale's mom.

"I'm ready!" said Mikale.

Mikale held his parents' hands tightly as they waded into the water. The ocean was very calm. Mikale felt safe. The waves gently rolled up over his tummy. The salty spray tickled his nose and made him laugh.

"One day you will dive into those waves and you won't be afraid," Uncle Mako told him. "Then we'll call you Keiki'la, just like your fish!"

Mikale beamed.

That night, Mikale told his fish all about his day in the ocean and his new nickname. Keiki'la went *bloop! bloop! bloop!* Mikale was sure that meant "I'm proud of you."

Aloha!